The Last Encounter

By Abhishek Roy Chowdhury

First published by
Evincepub Publishing
SMIG-65, Parijat Extension
Nehru Nagar Bilaspur, Chattisgarh 495001
Copyright © Abhishek Roy Chowdhury 2021
ISBN: 978-93-5446-114-9

This book is dedicated to my parents who provided support and guidance in every endeavour, to my wife who stood by me through thick and thin, and to my son who encouraged me to write this novel.

The Book

"The Last Encounter" is a work of fiction. The story is about a burglar, who planned a furtive operation to rob an empty house. As he broke into the house, he was taken aback to find that the family left for vacation leaving a lady, presumably their domestic help, enslaved in the house. He left the house that night, but his qualm of conscience compelled him to keep coming back to help the lady escape from the confinement. The girl's narrative full of misery made him empathetic towards her. The next evening, as he returned to the house for a last time to take the lady away, he was shocked to realize that the girl mysteriously disappeared from the locked building. However, he accidentally found a diary written by the girl revealing unknown and agonizing truth. The diary narrated how the family she worked for tortured her and always kept her enslaved in her room. The burglar, determined to find the girl, surrendered to the Police along with the diary. He also wanted to expose the family members that apparently ill-treated their maid. Eventually, the Police investigation discovered a spine-chilling truth that left everybody baffled.

The Author

Abhishek Roy Chowdhury was born and brought up in Kolkata. He had pursued Diploma in Business Management (New Delhi) and initially started his career in Kolkata. Later he moved to Hyderabad and has been staying there for last fifteen years. He has sixteen years of corporate experience and also holds an Executive General Management certification from IIM Calcutta.

Abhishek developed a passion for writing during his graduation days. He has been a business author and has published a series of articles and research papers in various magazines & journals. This is his first fiction, as now he aspires to reach a broader audience with his creativity.

You may reach out to the author at

abhishekrc@rediffmail.com

Contents

Chapter 1

The Plan

Dilip's furtive *"rendezvous"* usually begin very late into the nights. He never leaves home until the clock hits midnight. Before each operation, Dilip follows a specific routine. He finishes his so-called *dinner* little early in the evening. He absentmindedly gulps down the *chapathi* and tasteless vegetables. Then he re-arranges all his equipment in a small, shabby cotton bag that he carries on his back. This bag contains all essential tools for his work - a wire cutter, a metal rod, a knife, a set of keys of different shapes and sizes, and a heavy-duty torch that requires four cells. Then he puts on a black, skin-tight T-shirt and a dark-blue pair of jeans. Dark colours help him camouflage with the layers of the dark nights.

Finally, he lights-up a *bidi* and takes frequent but deep puffs. When it is right time to leave, he unlocks his bicycle that is as worn out as his old pair of jeans. Dilip checks the air-pressure of the tyres for one last time, wears the backpack on his back, takes a deep breath and leaves home for his pre-determined destination in the northern part of the town.

The process of identifying the right target is generally long and tedious. Dilip does a thorough scrutiny of the location and the house he selects. He collects all relevant information about the number of family members who permanently stay in the house, their standard of living, number of entry and exit points, appropriate time for sneaking in etc.; and carefully notes down every small detail in a little pocket book. This book has the entire history of all the petty crimes he has committed till date.

He also makes sure to not take the risk of performing his stealthy operations close to his locality. He chooses a location where nobody has a chance of recognizing him. He selects a house that poses the least amount of risk of getting caught. All these activities take days; at times weeks, before he narrows his options down to one target. Wrong information may lead to an incorrect decision that may prove to be fatal. Life does not always give a second chance, specifically in the risky profession Dilip is in.

*

Dilip was preparing for another such operation. Based on the information Dilip had been secretly collecting for the preceding ten days, he deliberately targeted a house that was not too far from his place. Definitely this was not his usual practice. He always felt a great sense of risk to break into buildings within a radius of two kilometres from his home.

However, this case was unique. This was a golden opportunity. With great difficulty he managed to find a house that was to remain entirely empty for four consecutive nights. He had inquired and gathered solid information that the whole family was away from home on vacation, keeping the house locked for almost the entire week. To successfully execute the work, Dilip targeted the second night in which the house would remain locked.

Nevertheless, Dilip never took chances. He never took uncalculated risks during his work. He didn't love surprises; particularly the unpleasant ones. He was aware that at times people had their close friends or relatives stay at their home temporarily, when they put up at another place overnight. Dilip actually sat in front of the locked main door and watched patiently for four long hours the previous night to ensure that nobody came to stay in the house. He made his mind up only when he was completely assured that the house was indeed empty and left unattended. The only cost he paid for that assurance was tolerating mosquito bites for four hours, though that was nothing compared to risking his own life due to ignorance. This was the reason for skipping the first night and targeting the second.

*

It was an old, two-storey building that was noticeably isolated from its neighbouring houses. The ground floor had a homeopathy shop and a dry-cleaning shop on the front side. The owners of the house, who stayed with family on the first floor, enjoyed a handsome amount of money as rents from both the shop owners. Needless to mention, both the shops remained shut after 8 P.M. in the evening. The main door was connected to a narrow passage that led to a staircase to reach the first floor. Now when the main door was locked, the only ideal way to reach the first floor was through the backside of the building. At the rear side of the house, there was a small garden covered with a tall tree and a few shrubs. That area was bounded by moderately high walls; thus no one standing in the garden could be seen from the houses nearby. From the garden, a drainage pipe led to a section on the first floor, dedicated for washing clothes and utensils. That part of the house was covered with a thin iron mesh. Many old houses in the town had similar layouts. Some of them didn't even have a net as an extra layer of protection.

This open area on the first floor was the most preferred option Dilip found to enter the house with a minimum hassle. There was a backdoor that connected the house with the backyard. That door was likely to remain locked from inside as nobody was at home. Breaking the door was not too difficult for Dilip, but that would definitely make a lot of noise, causing an alarm to the neighbours. As another option, it would have been easier to simply break the locks on the front door with his iron rod and enter. The risk was that while doing so, he could be too exposed under the street light that was right in front of the main door. Last month he had to abort his plan in a similar situation in another location, as the street dogs started barking loudly. That night, Dilip managed to run away in time and saved himself. Thus, climbing the pipe to reach the utility was the last but relatively the most secured option left.

Actually, Dilip was able to plan that immaculately as he had already done a thorough survey of the house in advance. He had visited that house owned by the *Kumar family* last week, in disguise of a plumber. Well, *disguise* might not be the right word to describe the activity. The *Kumar*s needed a plumber, and Dilip was a *real plumber* in broad daylight. Plumbing was a skill that he acquired from his father. Now, Dilip was quite in demand as a plumber in his neighbourhood. His fame was not only due to the scarcity of efficient plumbers in that area, but also because of his expertise in that work as a result of the legacy his father left for him. However, the *skill* that he mastered later; the *skill* that he exercised only when *darkness prevailed;* helped him earn the major portion of his living. He was the king of darkness. At least that was what he believed about himself.

Dilip quickly ran through the plan in his mind as he kept pedalling on his cycle through the deserted lanes. Another five minutes and he would be there. He knew exactly what to do. He had thought the plan through at least a million times. He just needed to reach the backyard of the building, climb up the drainage pipe a little to reach the *utility area* covered with thin metal nets at the first floor, cut the net with his tools and finally jump in…ought to be a smooth operation. He had climbed up multi-storey buildings many times in his life. Once he was in, entering the bedrooms was no big deal for a *pro* like Dilip, even if there were locks on each door. The L-shaped metal rod that he always carried with him for these operations was particularly for the purpose of breaking locks, in addition to be used for self-defence. Alternatively, he would try with the bunch of keys he had. One of them would fit in for sure. He had approximately four hours before dawn to finish his work. This would be a cakewalk. The only obstacles were the stray dogs which could create a chaos and ruin the plan. Overall, it was a safe plan, waiting to be executed successfully. Dilip felt more energized by this thought and increased his speed of pedalling. The cold wind and the clear night sky full of bright little stars really felt so stimulating.

Chapter 2

The Encounter

Around half past one, when the streets of the town were sleeping peacefully under a heavy blanket of thick darkness, Dilip stopped his cycle at the entrance of the lane. He hid his cycle in a dark corner in front of a closed *pan shop*. Then he looked around to ensure he was alone. When he was fully assured that he was not being watched by any sleepless eyes from any of the balconies around, he started walking towards the house he chose for the night. Dilip walked about fifty metres to reach the front door of the building. The house was the last one in this row and the lane had a *dead-end*. That kind of position was really advantageous for him as there was barely any chance of interruption by neighbours. However, the flip side was, if the situation went south, he would be left with only one way out of the lane. He was well aware of the danger. His job couldn't be completely risk free anyway.

There was a thin, short, partly broken wall of bricks as a partition on the left side of the building. Dilip easily jumped on the wall and walked silently like a cat, skilfully balancing himself. Quickly he reached the small garden at the backside of the house. He adjusted the bag on his shoulder and pulled his jeans up a little. The old pair of jeans always kept sliding down on his waist without a belt. He looked up at the place covered with the net. Without wasting much time, he started climbing on the pipe. This part of the game was also a part of most of his plumbing assignments. Being thin and flexible was the requirement for both day and night jobs for him. He climbed up to the spot in almost no time. Holding the pipe firmly with one hand, Dilip took out the wire-cutter from his hip-pocket with the other. Silently but swiftly, he began cutting the mesh. The mesh was a bit harder than he imagined it would be, but he could manage that. Being in that position was one of the riskiest parts of the work. He was not in the house yet. Thus, he still could be easily noticed; but then he was not in a state to escape either, even if he could sniff an upcoming danger. He was still hanging outside the first floor, balancing on the metal drainage pipe, completely exposed to the world.

Following significant effort, Dilip managed to cut the mesh, making a semi-circular opening. The hole was large enough for a person like him to sneak in. Still balancing on the pipe, Dilip pushed the broken part of the mesh to bend it towards inside. The broken edges were sharp. He needed to be careful. He looked around for one last time and carefully inserted one leg. He managed to reach a solid concrete base under his bare foot. Without delay, he pulled himself in and landed on the floor. There was an uncanny silence in the narrow but long passage in front of him. There were rooms on both sides of the narrow passage of this old-fashioned house. The largest bedroom was at the end of the hallway. That was his first target as per the plan. Dilip stepped forward to enter the passage. *At that very moment*, the sight at the other end of the corridor sent a chill down his spine. He was not alone in the house. HE WAS NOT ALONE!!!

*

There was a *silhouette* standing like a phantom at a distance of approximately ten feet from Dilip. Faint street lights entering the corridor through the air holes on the wall had made the sight really creepy. A suppressed cry came out of Dilip's mouth in dismay. He was stalled, unable to move an inch; as if his feet were glued to the ground. He was not sure how long he stood there, utterly speechless. Finally, he regained his composure. Within a fraction of a second, so many thoughts struck his mind. He had broken into myriad houses countless number of times. Many of those were empty houses. Some of those were vacant and locked for months together. Dilip was risk averse by nature. He preferred to choose empty houses. He never bumped into a ghost. He had been to places much scarier than the Kumars' empty building. Well, keeping his profession in mind, he did not give a damn about a ghost. Did that mean that his information failed him this time!...But the house was locked from outside. Then…how…how on earth was this possible?

The faint outline of the human figure was presumably of a woman. She was standing like a goddess in the darkness, with her hairs unrestrained. When Dilip visited the house last week for the plumbing work, there were only two women in the Kumar family. They were the two wives of the Kumar brothers. Naturally, both the ladies were now supposed to be away for the family vacation. Dilip did not have any information about a third woman in the house.

After a period of unnatural silence, the figure in the dark spoke in an obscure voice – "Who are you"? Her weak voice undoubtedly reflected the *fear of unknown*. Her words shook Dilip. Ghosts neither asked questions, nor were they frightened by the presence of human. He suddenly realized that he had a four-cell torch in his bag. He promptly took that out and flashed the light on the shadowy figure. The figure in the dark was immediately flooded with bright light. The lady covered her eyes with one hand against the sudden and sharp beam of light. Then she slowly lowered her hand as her eyes gradually got adjusted to the light. Dilip asked back like a zombie – "Who are you"?

The woman was in her mid-thirties. She had a dark complexion. A pale, shabby, yellow *saree* was wrapped around her body. Her hair was hanging loose over her stooping, narrow shoulders covered with a very ordinary blouse of pale green colour. Her eyes were still appearing completely startled. Her eyes were dark. Her eyes were deep. Her lips, still trembling in fear, replied – "I stay here".

Now it was Dilip's turn to be astounded. He fumbled, "But…but the house is locked, all have gone out for a week, I KNOW THAT." Dilip stressed on the last sentence, probably to reaffirm the validity of his information to himself. He was still struggling to come out of the sudden shock.

Before he could finish his lines, the woman nervously responded – "They locked me in." With a small pause she continued, "They always keep me locked in the house when they go out for days in a row".

"Please don't shout; I will leave. Please don't…", Dilip pleaded. His torch was also very heavy in addition to being heavy-duty. He held the heavy metal torch tightly in his right palm. In case she would shout, this torch would come in handy to silence her. He had no intention to harm anyone, unless pushed to the wall. Also, he never had hit women and children. He was only worried that the woman might make a noise to attract the neighbours' attention. He was still not sure if she was the only person left at home. The woman neither moved, nor spoke a word. She stood still in the dark. Undoubtedly, she was as terrified as Dilip was.

"Are you alone in the house?" Dilip asked inquisitively.

"I told you. They leave me here and put a lock on the main door when they leave home for a long time", said the woman. She was slowly beginning to breathe normally. Her voice sounded relatively stable now.

If she was the only living being in the house, it was of less danger to Dilip. Even if she would have shouted, it was unlikely to reach the nearest building. This house was significantly cut off from other houses in the lane. 'Well, if she had to shout, she would have probably done that by now', thought Dilip. Also, it did not seem like she had got company. The rest of the house was completely dark and extremely silent, with no sign of any existence of anyone else.

Dilip asked again, "so you work in this house?" No response came back from the woman. He was now feeling little uncomfortable by her silence. So, he continued, "What's your name?"

"Prabha", the woman replied.

Chapter 3

The Conversation

Both remained speechless for a few moments. Now the ghostly figure in the dark had a name and a face.

Prabha opened her mouth after the brief pause, "So, you are a thief!" It was not exactly a question. The tone was of apprehension.

"Don't be scared, I won't harm you", Dilip tried to reassure the woman. At the same time, he assured himself that there was nothing to be scared off. It was difficult to tell who among the two was scared more than the other.

"My name is Dilip", he said. He was not sure why he revealed his name. The woman did not ask for an introduction. In fact, this was not a situation to get introduced to each other formally. However, he kept talking - "I had information that nobody is at home for the full week. How would I know..." - Dilip stopped in the middle abruptly. Then he repeated, "I won't hurt you; don't worry."

"I am not worried. Why should I be? I have nothing to lose…but if you steal anything, they will put the blame on me when they come back".

Dilip sat on the floor and dropped the cotton bag beside him. The bunch of keys and the iron rod inside the bag made a loud metallic sound. Dilip's face was revealing a combination of disappointment and bewilderment at the same time.

"They keep you locked in the house for days! And it seems you accepted that! You never complained?" – asked Dilip.

Prabha slowly sat on the floor, resting against the wall of the passage. He was not sensing any threat any longer from the harmless looking poor woman sitting before him. Probably the woman was also not anticipating any danger from the stranger anymore. She was gazing at the floor and thinking something intensely. Then she spoke, "I have nowhere to go. They give me food, shelter, these clothes to wear. So, I don't try to flee. Earlier they used to lock me in a room for days whenever they left for a vacation. Now they have realized that I would not try to escape again. In fact, I can't escape now. Still they lock the main door from outside when they go out for days together, in case I conspire to rob the house and run away."

"What do you mean you would not escape again? Did you try to escape earlier?" Dilip asked curiously. No answer came from her as usual.

Malnutrition was evident in her poorly fed, nearly

emaciated appearance. She had innocence in her eyes though. Her face looked magical in the soft light entering in the corridor from the lamp post outside.

They were strangers to each other just a few moments back; but now both were slowly getting comfortable. Dilip continued talking, "This means, you will be locked in this house for three more days?"

"They have kept some food for me in the kitchen. I will somehow manage to survive with that", Prabha responded. There was no life in her voice.

Dilip asked, "Are you hungry?" Prabha remained silent again. Each time Dilip left home to carry out his plans at night, he always carried some food in his bag. He always felt hungry when he stayed up in the night. He took out a small packet of biscuits and tossed it towards Prabha. Without any sign of hesitation, she picked it up, tore the packet and started munching the biscuits like a starving child. A heavenly satisfaction was visible on her innocent face.

"You said they keep food for you? It doesn't seem like you ate anything in last twenty four hours." Dilip commented observing the intensity she was eating with.

Prabha did not answer and kept eating. She finished the whole packet of biscuits before Dilip could blink. Then she wiped her mouth with the *anchal* of her *saree*. Finally, she said, "Whatever they have kept for me, should last for the next three days. I need to consume wisely. I can afford to have only one meal a day."

Food in her stomach has put life back into her soul. Food does wonders to hungry stomach. Who knows better than Dilip! Hunger always accompanied him throughout his childhood. Even now, he did not have steady earnings. He always spent days in planning. Then usually after a long wait, one successful execution of his plan brought some fortune for him, only to last for a few days. He bought his rations and stored for rainy days. He was probably as poor as this girl. The only significant difference was – Dilip was free, and the girl was captive.

Dilip had a plan to buy chicken and cook for himself after this operation at the Kumar's house. He got to savour the taste of such delight only once in a blue moon. He also had thought of buying a pack of cigarettes as he almost had forgotten the taste of cigarettes. He was tired of smoking *bidis* for months. Unfortunately, after this failed attempt, it seemed he was still not destined to have such *kismet*.

Still, he was feeling warm inside. This was an unfamiliar feeling for him. He was unable to decipher his feelings. He had never been generous to anyone. In fact, he had never cared for anyone. For some unknown reason, the helplessness of the woman that he came across by mere accident, created a maudlin moment that he was just unable to brush off.

"Where do you stay?", asked Prabha.

"Not far", Dilip threw a short answer at her. It was not safe to disclose more; definitely not at this stage. It was probably too early to trust a stranger, who crossed his path in a bizarre way that was beyond his wildest imagination. Also, he needed to remember that he was not too far from his locality.

Dilip suddenly realised that he was probably wasting time sitting there. The night was not going to be fruitful at all. He needed to plan again, for some other place, some other day. He again needed to spend days finding a lead. A delicious meal now would have to wait for days. He also knew, spending more time there might create more peril for him. Talking more would have revealed more about him, increasing the risk.

However, at the same time, he also felt that those thoughts about the unsuccessful operation were not really bothering him. He was struggling to understand the reason for the discomfort within him. Was it simply his failure to make the plan work? Or was it the awkward moment of getting caught in that unusual situation? Or…was it the helpless condition of the woman sitting in a feeble manner in front of him.

It was probably the first instance in his life when his soul was feeling a strong urge inside to help someone. Dilip grabbed the bag and stood up. Then he said in a husky voice, "I can set you free from captivity. I can break the locks on the main door and let you flee."

Surprisingly, Prabha did not seem to be thrilled by this idea at all. Instead, she looked up and said in an indifferent tone, "And when they come back, they would reach out to the police to find me. You would also get caught in this affair. Neither I need additional trouble in my life, nor do I want to put your life in danger. You won't have to think about me. Leave me alone."

Dilip kept looking at her face in surprise for a few moments. He had no idea how the woman who lived a life full of misery could turn down an offer to be released from the confinement. Her eyes had an unearthly aura. Her eyes had something that compelled Dilip to restrain himself from insisting. Without more delay, he turned back and swiftly reached the area of the broken mesh, through which he had entered the house. With some effort, he got through the hole and quickly reached for the pipe. Getting in was always easier than getting out through a broken net. He climbed down the pipe like a monkey. He wore his sandals that he left in the backyard and without spending a single moment he ran to his cycle. In almost no time, Dilip disappeared into the darkness of the cold, foggy night. There was a very unusual heaviness in his chest; one that he was not at all familiar with.

Chapter 4

The Compunction

Dilip awoke very late in the morning. He could not immediately recall the incident of the last night. He sat on the bedstead for some time to reorganize his thoughts. Slowly he managed to regain his faculties. He looked at his old wristwatch. It was close to eleven in the morning. He jumped out of his *chaarpai* and immediately started to get ready. He was supposed to attend *Basu* uncle's house for some petty plumbing work. Mr. *Basu* had been calling him since last few days for a small work that Dilip was hardly interested in. These were regular work for him that hardly earned a good living. Also, attending the houses in Dilip's own locality could barely open the door for any opportunities to grab additional wealth.

Still, he could not stop doing the job of a plumber. At least, those small assignments gave him a steady income, even if those were small amounts. Dilip's father struggled through his entire life, depending only on that profession.

Dilip did not want the same life he had experienced since childhood. He desperately needed a better life – better food to eat, better clothes to wear and last but not the least, a better wife who would not leave her children and run away due to the incapability of her husband to provide good food for at least two times a day.

The disappointment of last night left him completely baffled. In spite of a clean pre-work, he failed to gather complete information. How could it be possible for him to know that those scoundrels kept their maid in confinement and left to enjoy a family vacation for days! How could those educated and so-called sophisticated families treat people like that! He had read about similar inhumane incidents in the news papers; but never had imagined that he would come across one in his life one day.

But then, how come he did not capture this information earlier! He got the lead from his reliable sources. They never mentioned anything about a domestic help leaving in that house. He visited the house earlier and never noticed anything. He spent hours standing in that lane where *Kumar's* house was situated, secretly watching each member of the family. Kumar brothers and their families stayed together in that house. There were two brothers in their forties, their wives and their children. He had seen each of them leaving home for work or school and coming back at different times of the day. He never saw a maid entering or coming out of the house in last two weeks. It looked as if she never existed. Probably they never let her out fearing she might run away.

*

Dilip came back home around two in the afternoon, after finishing his plumbing work. He got some money to manage his meals for the day. He had his afternoon meal at *Ranu Mausi's dhaba* in his lane while returning. He was a regular customer there. For underprivileged bachelors like him, who could afford only *roti-sabzi* as regular meals, those cheap local *dhabas* came as saviour.

Dilip started smoking a *bidi* lying down on his cot. This was his personal time to think, plan and introspect. Today his mind was quite disturbed though. A failed plan messed up the entire schedule he had chalked out. His plan for *chicken and rice* had gone for a toss anyway. He might not be able to see any sign of fortune in the next few weeks.

However, the uneasiness in his mind was actually due to something else. He was struggling to cope with a feeling of guilt inside. Unfortunately, he was unable to make out the reason for the same. It was not his fault that the poor girl was locked in the house out there. Probably it was his powerlessness to help her in any way!

Throughout the morning, he visualized the woman sitting alone at the empty house. Had she been feeling hungry! Did she have enough to eat for the day; the only meal she could afford each day! Dilip already started to consider himself as a selfish person to leave her alone, inhumanly locked in that house. But then, what else could he have done! He offered to help her but she refused – Dilip tried to convince himself.

Dilip stayed home for the rest of the day. His mind kept juggling with dilemma. Keeping the illicit way of earning his living in mind, he always preferred to stay away from unwanted trouble and did not meddle in matters that did not directly concern him. As a matter of fact, an unknown girl in a distant house in one corner of the town had no significant reason to make him feel that way. After all, that was not the first time Dilip heard of such irresponsible act by wealthy families that treated their domestic help in a torturous way.

*

At times, Dilip cooked food for himself. Preparing food at home was always a cheaper option than buying ready-made meal from outside - specifically in the kind of situation he was in when he had no hope to see any inflow of cash in the next few days; or actually weeks. He had nothing planned for the near future. Planning for each operation usually took at least two weeks, provided he got reliable information from the trusted sources. Moreover, good planning needed motivation and a clear mind to think. Both were absent at the moment for him.

With great lethargy, Dilip managed to prepare *chapathi and sabzi* in the evening. Then he finished his meal around nine. He did not have a TV. Drinking cheap rum was the only activity that gave some solace to him during each evening, sitting alone in his so-called home. Surprisingly, he was not even feeling like drinking at the moment. He was absent minded throughout the day. Still lost in his thoughts, he washed his utensils like a machine, sitting under the municipality tap in front of his *jhopri*.

Then he sat on the ground and lit a *bidi*. Whenever Dilip had run out of cash, he stopped buying cigarettes and started smoking *bidi*. He always smoked the last *bidi* of the day with relish. He made it a practice to put all his worries away for those five minutes at the end of each day. With each puff he inhaled life into his soul and exhaled all the anguish and frustration out of his mind, at least for the night. To him, it felt like meditation that made him calm for some time. Then he preferred to immediately go to sleep with a peaceful mind, keeping all worries and uncertainties of tomorrow at bay. Tomorrow was always a new day with a fresh hunt for food.

But that night was different. The night seemed longer than usual. Dilip was not enjoying the unusual *qualm of conscience* within him. His mind was restless. He was unable to think clearly due to the clatter of contradicting thoughts inhis mind.

Finally, Dilip gave in to the dilemma after a day-long struggle. He threw the *bidi* away and got up. He, then quickly packed two extra *chapathis* that he prepared and stored for the next morning and the leftover *sabzi* in a small tiffin box. He swiftly put on the only pair of jeans he had. Holding the tiffin box in hand, Dilip came out of his hut. He locked the partly broken door and unlocked the chain on the cycle. He silently started pedalling and soon reached the main road. His was now able to clear the fog in his mind.

Now, he was feeling content. He was feeling warm. He felt that kind of warmth inside for the first time in his life.

Chapter 5

The Return

Dilip never visited the same place twice. He never revisited a house he had broken in once even in the distant past. Today, for the first time in his life, he returned to the same house that he broke into just the previous night. Even Dilip was unsure of the reason of such exception that he allowed to himself.

However, there was an advantage of visiting a known place. Entry and exit were lot smoother than the first time. There were less issues to take care of. It took Dilip only a few moments to follow the same path he already walked the other night. The net was already broken near the utility area on the first floor. Therefore, no additional work was required. No unexpected challenges were there to address. He silently stepped into the corridor and moved forward in the dark. Dilip passed by the locked bedrooms, the kitchen and finally reached the last room in the row. The door was ajar. He stopped for a moment in front of the door and peeked into the room. In dim light, he could see the woman lying on the floor. She had her *pallu* wrapped around her like a blanket. Around that time of the year, temperature at night usually started dropping. Her womanly curves were more prominent in the dusky light entering through a small glass window. He felt hesitant to enter; but then, that was the woman he had come for in the middle of the night. That was the woman who drove him to take the same risk twice.

He pushed the door and entered the room. Prabha was probably not in deep sleep. With the creak of the door, she opened her eyes. She then looked up and found Dilip standing in front of her. The natural expression Dilip expected from her was of surprise and disbelief. In fact, she should have been significantly terrified finding him in the house again at that hour of night. Definitely Prabha had no reason to expect him to be back, unless he had a bad intention.

To his surprise, Prabha did not show any sign of fright in her movement. She slowly sat up, adjusting her *saree*. She might be a little embarrassed as she was not prepared for this. Any woman would have been embarrassed to be seen sleeping with her clothes not properly organized. It seemed Prabha anticipated his return. Dilip had an uneasy smile on his face. He was unsure how to begin. Prabha looked straight at him with sleepy eyes and said in a raspy voice, "Why did you come back?" Oh…those eyes. Those dark and large eyes were in clear contrast to her body. Dilip had noticed them on the very first night.

There was hoarseness in her voice as she was sleeping. There was no chair or bed in the room. Prabha was sleeping on an old, torn mat. The colour of the mat was so faded that it was impossible to tell if it was red or yellow when it was new. There was an unfamiliar odour in the room.

Dilip slowly sat on one side of the mat – "Yes, I came back". He was struggling to find words. He was also feeling a little uneasy that he gave this surprise to her. He paused andcontinued, "I don't understand why you are not trying to run away when I am here to help. They would come back in two days and will find the broken net beside the utility area. They would anyway come to know about my intrusion during their vacation. How would you explain that to them?"

Dilip realised this part only last night. The broken part of the net would raise a lot of questions. The owners would demand an explanation from Prabha, as she was the only one in the house. In fact, he thought out a narrative for Prabha to justify that, in case she refused to run away before they came back. Prabha could tell them about the entry of a thief; but then the thief realised the presence of the woman in the house. To be on the safer side he gave up and retreated through the same route that he came in, before she could make a noise. The story did not have much deviation from the truth, except that in reality the thief actually sat and chattered with Prabha for some time before leaving the house. Needless to mention, that part was not to be told to her masters.

However, Dilip already decided that before he would give the idea to Prabha, he would try his best to convince her to break away from that hell. Dilip was about to open his mouth; when Prabha spoke up indifferently, "If you are worried about how I would explain this, why don't you go and fix the net".

Dilip didn't know what to say. He kept looking at her face like a dullard. Prabha continued, "I can explain the broken net, as long as I stay back. If I run away, the situation will be worse. They will put the tag of a burglar on me as well. Then both will be caught and thrashed. Why do you want to invite more trouble for a woman like me?"

Prabha's face was looking dry and pale. She was appearing weaker than she was the previous night. Dilip suddenly realised that he was still holding the tiffin carrier in his hand. He rolled the round carrier on the floor towards Prabha.

"I got some food for you. Have it quickly", Dilip said briefly.

Prabha already might have noticed the box in his hand but was not sure if there was food in it. Probably she was waiting for Dilip to give it to her. She was hungry for sure. She did not wait for another moment. Prabha immediately opened the box and started eating the food. Even the taste of cold *chapathi and sabzi* seemed heavenly when one was hungry. Dilip sat patiently and watched her eating. Hunger makes one forget the entire world. Dilip was more than familiar with the feeling of starvation since his childhood.

When she was done eating, Dilip started speaking again. He needed to induce her to leave that house. He continued, "What would you tell them about the broken net? Would anybody believe that a thief came and left without stealing anything from the house! Also, would they believe the thief left you unharmed!"

"But that's the reality; at least till now", replied Prabha. Then she thought something for a few moments and said with suspicion in her tone, "have you come back with the intention to rob the house now?"

"No, I have not." In Dilip's voice, it was more of desperation to make her believe, than the assurance. He continued, "If I had to rob, I would have done that yesterday itself. I had the scope."

"Then what brought you here again?" Prabha seemed curious.

Dilip started arranging the pieces of the tiffin carrier together, while organizing the words in his mind. He never expressed his emotions openly to anyone since childhood; specifically not to a woman. He was never in close association of any woman. Finally, he managed to speak his mind with great difficulty.

Dilip started, "I thought a lot after I went back yesterday. I felt that I could have helped you, but I did nothing. I only thought about myself and ran away. But then, my conscience forced me to come back here. I am a criminal, but I still have humanity alive in me. I can't leave you with those people who treat you in such inhumane way."

Prabha forced a smile on her gloomy face. She never heard words of kindness from anyone for years. She was not habituated being cared for. Probably she was struggling to decide how she could react to this. After remaining silent for a few moments, she started speaking with a grim expression on her face – "I have faced much more than you know, or you can imagine. You know almost nothing about me!"

Dilip immediately said, "I want to know. I am here to help you. I could have moved on and simply forget about you; but my conscience did not allow me to stay aloof." As he completed these sentences, he noticed tears rolling down Prabha's eyes.

Chapter 6

The Revelation

Prabha poured her heart out to Dilip that night. Surprisingly, she revealed a lot about her past to a person, who could still be considered just a stranger. An accidental encounter, followed by an unexpected return of the man the next day, did not necessarily make him a friend to reveal everything to. In spite of knowing that, Prabha could still open up to Dilip as she had started feeling a connection and a sense of togetherness with Dilip. This was probably because both were deprived and destitute. Both had nothing to lose.

Prabha told her story. She had studied till 7th standard in her village. Her parents died in an accident when she was only sixteen. The only distant relative she had was an aunt, who lived in the neighbouring village. That aunt brought her to the town to help her find work. Since then, she had been working in various places as a domestic help. Just two years back she came to the Kumar family to work as a full-time maid. Since she had joined the family, she experienced only pain and misery.

Prabha survived with minimal food every day. She was already sleep-deprived. She was often beaten by the house owners for trivial mistakes. Many times, she spent days together locked-up in the room, without food and water. She was never allowed to leave the house. Prabha also disclosed that once she tried to escape; but was caught. She was stripped and tortured by the family members for hours in her room. Since then, she lost her courage to even attempt to run away. There was no light of hope left for her.

Prabha also mentioned that every night she used to write her experiences in a small notebook. She was not much educated, but literate enough to write her story in the diary that she kept in a secret place in her room, hidden from her *malik*. As she was not allowed to talk to anyone, writing down her experiences every night gave her some solace. This was Prabha's narration of her life in a nutshell.

It sounded like a fiction from a crime story book. He always thought these stories were only at times heard from others but were never seen in reality. He never imagined that he would actually come across a real victim of such crimes in his life.

After hearing the entire narrative, Dilip had to put significant effort convincing her to run away. She had been refusing Dilip's help since the beginning as she had no place to go to and no one to be considered as close relative or friend in the town. Dilip assured her that he could arrange some place at any other part of the town as a temporary hideout. He could not take the risk of keeping Prabha in his *jhopri* as that could create suspicion among the people around.

Most likely, that family would return home and lodge a police complaint, finding their maid had gone missing. The locks on the main door would be found broken too. It was definitely not possible for the woman to climb down the pipe like Dilip did. Therefore, breaking the locks on the main door was the only option to let her out of the house Also, the net at the back-side utility area was already damaged. The presence of an unknown woman at Dilip's place overnight, in addition to a missing complaint of a maid in the neighbourhood, would be a deadly combination for them. After all, this house was not miles away from Dilip's slum. It would be safe to be away from his usual location for a few days.

Dilip came home few minutes before sunrise last night. He had a sense of accomplishment in his heart. He was able to make Prabha finally agree to break out of the dirty rut she had been stuck in for years. It was not that she was fully convinced; but at the end, she stopped saying 'No'.

However, with that sense of satisfaction, Dilip also had an additional responsibility now. He had only one day to find out a place for Prabha; or may be, for both. He and Prabha planned to escape at night. Only the last night was left for them before the Kumar family members returned from the vacation.

Dilip could have insisted her to run away last night itself, as he had already taken the risk of sneaking in for the second time into the building. Unfortunately, he was not sure about a safe shelter. Therefore, he would need to go in again, for the third and the last time. Prabha promised to be ready with her belongings. She did not have a lot to carry. She had an old suitcase that contained all her stuff.

Dilip did not want to waste time now. He had a lot to do before dusk. He needed to pack some necessary stuff if he really had to be underground for some days following the escape. He threw the *bidi* and got up. Then he quickly started packing all his essential items in a large side bag. He did not want to make it heavy though.

When he was done with packing all the necessary belongings, he took his cycle to the local cycle shop. He got the old tyres refilled with air. Then he finished buying some vegetables and *atta*. He needed to cook food for the night for two.

However, before preparing meal for the night, he had the most important work to do. It was important to find a home, preferably far from Dilip's slum. It was not easy to finda cheap rented place within a day in the town. He could not afford staying in a hotel. Also, hotel was not a safe option for them. The police would probably look for them in the relatively inexpensive hotels around the rail station.

*

Dilip struggled to find a solution the entire day. He roamed around the town on his cycle for the entire afternoon in search of a rented house. Unfortunately, he returned home with no luck in the evening. He had anticipated that finding an inexpensive room in the town in one day was not going to be easy.

He started making the meal, but his mind remained busy thinking. He still had few hours to decide. Finally, by the evening, one idea struck his mind. The only feasible and likely the safest option he found was to leave the town, at least for the time being. If he and Prabha could move at least a hundred miles away from the town overnight, chances of getting caught could be negligible. They could come back later after the initial rattle following their escape was over. He made up his mind.

The plan now was to take Prabha out of the house and directly reach the railway station. He knew that there were a few express trains that stopped at the local station at night for a few moments. They would get onto one of those. The general compartments would do. It really did not matter where it would take them but breaking free and not getting caught were the only priorities he had now.

This thought gave him some relief amidst a lot of uncertainty. 'After all, life is so uncertain', thought Dilip. He let out a sigh mixed with both hope and anxiety. He knew how his life took a turn during last three days and got him entangled in such a dilemma. Three days back, he broke into a house with a simple plan to rob the house, like he had done a million times earlier. And now he was preparing to leave the town with a nearly unknown girl, not knowing what the future had in store for them. More surprisingly, for the first time, he was taking a chance with his life for a person he did not yet know properly. 'Life is so unpredictable', murmured Dilip, completely sunk in his thought.

Chapter 7

The Disappearance

There were two locks on the main door. The door was little old fashioned and did not have an internal locking system. Kumar's residence was not a building with modern facilities. If the two locks were broken, there was no other obstruction to cross in order to enter the house. Dilip had already checked the locks. It would be easy to break the locks with an iron rod than trying to unlock those with the *fit-for-all* bunch of keys he had. Generally, he used the bunch of different types of keys to open locks that were difficult to break. That would be a time taking job to apply each key one by one to find which one was the right fit. That kind of effort was fruitful for opening a locker or an almirah. At Kumar's house, he needed to complete the entry part quickly as this time it was supposed to be a front door entry to the building. He could not afford to spend a lot of time standing in front of the main door, completely exposed under the street light.

Dilip stood quietly a few meters away from the door at a dark corner in the lane for some time, in order to ensure that nobody was watching. It was getting colder each night. In small towns, people preferred to go to bed early as mercury kept dropping rapidly every night during the fall. That was good for him in a way. He needed quieter nights to do his work. The only difficult part was standing out under the open sky during the colder nights.

Dilip appeared to be fortunate today. The streetlight in front of the main door was not on for some unknown reason. Probably it was fused. The building was standing like a huge black monster in the dark. Dilip took out the metal rod from his bag and moved to the door. He inserted the smaller arm of the L-shaped lever and held the end of the longer arm firmly with two hands. Then, one sudden jolt with his expert hands making a loud thudding sound broke the first lock. He stood silently for a few moments. He looked up at the nearest building. No…no lights were on. Nobody was leaning out from the balcony to check. He took a deep breath and focussed on the second lock. One last jerk with the metal rod and…Bingo! The job was done almost effortlessly. Dilip threw the broken locks to the bush near the main door and pushed the door open. Then he swiftly entered the house with his bag on his shoulder and closed the door without making any sound. He was finally in the house without any trouble. What a relief…at least for the time being!

The staircase was on the left. Dilip climbed the stairs rapidly and reached the first floor. Climbing stairs felt so convenient than climbing drainage pipes. He looked at the broken net on the other end of the house. 'Let it be like this' he thought. 'Let the assholes discover that someone broke in and took their maid away. Or let them imagine that the maid herself had cut the net and escaped. By the time the Police would start searching for them, they would be miles away.

As he entered through the front door this time, he was now standing on the other side of the corridor. Dilip dropped the heavy side bag on the floor and entered the corridor. It was extremely dark inside as the streetlight was not working. Not even a single ray of light was entering through the air holes. There was an eerie silence throughout the house. The moderately long corridor was looking like a dark and creepy tunnel. Dilip lit the flashlight. A third visit to the same place had made him comfortable now. He reached in front of Prabha's room and knocked on the door.

Dilip called her name standing outside the door – "Prabha!!!" No response came from inside. 'Ah!!! She must have fallen asleep', thought Dilip. The previous night Dilip told her not to sleep tonight. She was supposed to keep her bag packed and be ready to leave without wasting any time. They had planned to reach the station before 3:00 in the morning. An express train always stopped at the station around 3:15 A.M. Dilip planned to catch that train and reach far away before anybody realised anything. The owners were not scheduled to be back before evening the next day. The shop owners at the ground floor were likely to keep their shops shut down for at least two days. Diwali was round the corner. Everybody preferred to visit their hometowns around this time of the year. Those two shop owners were not local people, as far as Dilip had inquired. Therefore, they were not expected to be seen around the house for next few days. It was only people like Dilip or Prabha who had nowhere to go to during festivals.

Dilip called again, "Prabha!!!" This time he was a little louder, but still no answer from behind the closed door. Dilip could not wait any longer. He was not entering as he did not want to embarrass her again. Now, he had no choice. Dilip pushed the door open and entered the room. Prabha was not in the room. There was nobody in the room.

'She must be in the toilet', thought Dilip. He stood there in the middle of the room, waiting for Prabha to return. There was no suitcase around. It looked like nobody was staying in the room for last couple of weeks. The room was not like that yesterday. It was moderately clean last night. Now, there was dust on the floor. There was dust on everything. The mat which Prabha slept on was nowhere. How could the room collect dust in just 24 hours!

Dilip came out of the room and walked towards the bathroom. The door was shut. He knocked on the door and waited. No sound came from inside at all. He waited for few more seconds, hesitant to enter. Then he pushed the door and it opened. Inside it was complete darkness with no sign of anyone. All other rooms were locked. The only other place Prabha could be was on the terrace. Dilip ran to the terrace frantically…but alas! There was no sign of Prabha there as well. He came back to Prabha's room in a frenzy.

As he again entered the room in the dark, he stumbled upon something hard. Dilip flashed his torch on the ground. There was an old notebook lying on the ground. It was not there when he came to the room few moments back!!! If it would have been there, he would have noticed it for sure. He had waited in the room for almost over five minutes for Prabha earlier. Dilip's mind stopped working. His throat was dry. He picked up the notebook with a trembling hand.

The diary was old with a faded black cover. The pages had turned pale yellow. Dilip flipped first few pages. A photograph in black & white fell on the ground from the notebook. Dilip picked it up. It was a photo of Prabha in her younger age. However, her face was easily recognizable. There was no doubt that the notebook belonged to Prabha. She already mentioned about a diary to Dilip the previous night. She said that she wrote about the tortures she faced each day in the diary.

Dilip was miserably perplexed now. He was unable to figure out where she could have disappeared from a house that was locked outside. He was clueless about how the notebook appeared from nowhere in the middle of the room. Who left the notebook? When? Why?

To check one last possibility, Dilip ran to the broken net through which he had entered twice. He examined the hole very closely. It was impossible for Prabha to get through that, with a suitcase in hand. It was not a feasible option for a lady unless she was a professional and was habituated with that kind of escape routes. It took months of practice for Dilip to master those skills.

Dilip suddenly started feeling unsteady. He was unable to think anything any longer. He was feeling weak to stand on his feet. Dilip came back to the room with the notebook in his hand. He picked up his bag with a shaking hand. Then he climbed down the stairs slowly like a drunken man. He came out of the main door, lost in another world. Somehow, Dilip managed to reach the place where he kept the cycle. Few meters of walk from the door to that spot felt like few miles. He started pedalling on the cycle like a machine. The night suddenly felt a lot darker to his eyes. It felt like someone was hammering inside his head. The chirping sound of the crickets in the silence of the night seemed louder than ever.

Chapter 8

The Surprise

The train arrived very late, as usual. The Kumar brothers and their family returned after five days and four nights of refreshing but tiring vacation. Short vacations always involved a lot of commutes. Praveen and Naveen, the two brothers, hurriedly took out all the luggage and dumped on the platform. The train was scheduled to stop at the station for only three minutes. There was a huge pile of suitcases and trolley bags on the platform now.

Sarita and Deepa stood on the platform with their kids. The two kids were still in a vacation mode. Their minds were refusing to come out of the dreamworld that they had seen during the holidays. However, the two women did not look happy. They had already started complaining about coming back to the same old rut of household chores. Deepa, wife of Naveen, seemed more discontent.

"Didi, I have been insisting on finding a maid for last two weeks, but neither Naveen nor *Bhaiya* pay any attention", Deepa grunted.

Sarita was about to say something; but before she could respond, Praveen and Naveen came back to the platform. They had found a taxi, fortunately. Finding a taxi in the town at the late hours was really a matter of luck. They picked up the heavier luggage and started walking fast towards the exit gate. The women and the children followed reluctantly with relatively lighter bags and purses hanging from their hands. None of them were able to relish a feeling of coming back to home after a week. The *'home, sweet home'* feeling was not present; at least the expressions on their faces did not reveal contentment.

The lane was too narrow for sedans to enter. The driver refused to go till the main door of the house as the lane had a dead-end. It was nearly impossible to come out of the lane without hitting a wall or the lamp post. The Kumar family had to get down at the entry of the lane. The two brothers unloaded the luggage and then paid the fare to the cab driver. The driver disappeared with his car as soon as he got paid. As they picked up the heavy bags and started walking towards their home, Deepa screamed at the top of her lungs – "WHERE ARE THE LOCKS???"

Sarita and Deepa stood in front of the main door, absolutely thunderstruck. The Kumar brothers dropped the luggage on the spot. They ran towards the ladies immediately and joined them. They had the same reaction too. The two locks that they had put on the main door had disappeared. The door was left partly open.

"Someone has broken in", murmured Praveen to himself.

"Of course, someone has broken in. Now, what are you waiting for? Get in fast and check", Sarita lashed out at Praveen.

Praveen was still hesitating to enter, "What if someone is still in there?"

Sarita was impatient now, "Then you people stay here but I am going in the house".

The two men came to senses and rushed in, pushing the door wide open with a loud sound. They climbed up the stairs and in no time, they reached the first floor. Praveen ran for the bedrooms first. Naveen was about to follow. Accidentally his eyes fell on the net in the utility. He slowly walked towards the broken net. It had a hole, big enough to let a person in. The women and the kids had already reached the first floor by then. Naveen shouted, "*Bhaia*, look at this." Praveen was back at the spot, looking in the direction of the broken net. His face looked completely confused and terrified.

Sarita asked, "What did you see inside?"

"Nothing…all the locks are fine on the bedrooms. Nobody is in."

The two women ran to the corridor. To their surprise, they found that the locks on the respective bedrooms were hanging from the doors as they were supposed to be. Deepa took out the keys from her purse and opened the locks of the bedroom doors and the drawing room. Both hurriedly entered their respective bedrooms. The rooms looked intact, as they were left five days back. Not a single object had moved from its place.

The first thing the women checked was the almirah. Each of the bedrooms had an old-fashioned steel almirah with locker. They opened the almirah and unlocked the lockers. Nowadays nobody dared to keep a lot of jewellery and cash at home. Nevertheless, they still had enough at home to be stolen. All were there as they were kept in the respective lockers. They checked twice and all seemed to be untouched.

The women came back to the utility area where Kumar brothers were still standing, speculating over the broken net. It was clear to them that someone had sneaked in through the hole on the net. Probably the same culprit broke the locks on the main door. However, they were unable to understand why a thief had broken in and then left the house without stealing anything. That house had enough for a thief to get richer.

There was another puzzle to solve. If the culprit had broken the locks on the main door and entered the building, why was the net broken in the utility? Again, if the thief came through the hole that he made on the net in the utility, who broke the locks on the main door and why? Also, if the intruder was able to break the heavy locks on the main door, the locks on the bedroom doors would have been much easier to crack. There was enough time to accomplish the mission without any interruption. Fortunately, the intruder left the rooms untouched, that was really unbelievable.

All four of them were utterly confused now. They were clueless about the motive of a kind hearted thief who broke in but took nothing. They are wondering whether one person or more than one entered the house. The men looked at their respective wives in apprehension. They had mixed feelings. In one hand they were happy that nothing was stolen. On the other, they were still not out of the shock. Nobody could like that kind of surprises right after returning from a nice vacation.

Sarita finally opened her mouth, "We need to inform the Police". There was again an uneasy silence. The other three looked at each other. Deepa said, "Well, nothing is stolen. Why to involve the Police then?"

"That is even more suspicious. We need to know who the intruder was. Moreover, we need to know the motive", Sarita commented. "Don't you people find it absolutely funny for a burglar to leave without stealing anything? Even the flower vast we have in the drawing room could have been sold for at least a few thousands."

"Is it someone from Prabha's...", Deepa didn't complete her sentence.

"How is Prabha coming into picture here? She is gone." Naveen almost shouted.

"Well, that's not impossible Naveen", exclaimed Praveen.

Sarita said looking at her husband, with clear annoyance and command in her tone, "Let's not waste time arguing amongst us. Now will you go to the Police or you want me to go at this hour?"

The two men looked at each other helplessly. They made some faint attempt to convince Sarita, but she was determined to call the Police. As the men in the house were indecisive, the women naturally took charge of almost everything. Sarita was a dominating lady. The two men preferred to follow and not argue. Finally, the brothers moved to the staircase reluctantly. Nobody ever wanted to be involved the Police unless it was absolutely necessary. People always avoided Police; specifically, when they had enough to hide.

Chapter 9

The Diary

Earlier on the same day, Dilip had reached back home from Kumar's place well before the sunrise. It was still dark then. The town was yet to wake up. He threw the bag to one corner of his room and immediately took out the diary he accidentally found at Prabha's room in the Kumar's residence. He could not wait any longer to discover the content written in the diary. Since morning he had been exploring the diary. He skipped his meals. He did not go out of his room throughout the day. He did not feel like doing anything else except reading the diary.

Last night, standing in Prabha's room in a state of panic, Dilip could not have a good look at the diary. Back at his *jhopri*, he then had the entire day to go through each page, in the privacy of the four walls. He lit a *bidi* and picked up the book. The notebook was old, definitely had been used for a long time. He turned the black cover and Prabha's photo appeared again. He picked up the photograph. It was of younger Prabha; might be in her twenties. The face was not much different then. Anybody could be able to recognize her by having a glance at the photo. The only difference Dilip noticed was that she looked prettier and healthier in the picture. Dilip kept the photo aside and focussed on the notebook.

The handwriting seemed really unclear and hard to decipher at the beginning. Prabha's handwriting looked like a child's writing in kindergarten who struggled to write each letter. Reading and comprehending the content was really difficult for someone like Dilip, with limited literacy. However, he did not have a choice. He decided to read it. He really wanted to solve the mystery. He was determined to go till the end and uncover the truth.

Dilip noticed that each page had a date at the top. Dilip began reading from the first page that dated back to two years. Prabha probably started writing this after joining Kumar's house as a domestic help. The dates made it easier to understand the timeline. After significant effort Dilip made his way through the chapters that described Prabha's experiences in Kumar's residence for two years. The dates that were skipped while writing, revealed that Prabha did not write her experience each day; but each page narrated the misery and agony she faced while working for the Kumar family.

In a nutshell, the content in the diary uncovered that Prabha was provided with a small room beside the kitchen when she joined. She was given an old mat and a pillow as hard as a rock to sleep. Apparently, the family members, specifically the two ladies of the Kumar family, did not seem to be friendly and accommodating to Prabha. Their behaviour was somewhat rude from day one.

Dilip kept reading. The dates on the next few pages indicated that Prabha did not write for a couple of days. There was a gap of four to five days between each page. The content gradually revealed that Prabha had already started feeling uncomfortable staying with the family in the first week of her stint. Nobody had been treating her fairly since she came in the house. She was instructed to wake up very early in the morning and start with cleaning the kitchen and the passage. Before the family members woke up, she was supposed to keep their breakfast ready. The entire morning was being spent in cooking. In the afternoon she had her meal with limited quantity and items. She was served with *Daal-Roti* only. At times she was lucky to get some leftover *sabzi* as an additional dish to eat. The family members had other items in their lunch. They were non-vegetarians, but Prabha was never offered any of those dishes.

After this there was a long gap of about a month as per the date on the next age. Dilip lit another *bidi* and resumed reading the next page. Prabha was still working tirelessly. The men in the house used abusive languages at her very often. Prabha also mentioned that the younger brother, Naveen, used to leer at Prabha all the time. When his wife was not around, he also touched her on wrong places in a lascivious manner. She was scared whenever Naveen was around.

As Dilip continued reading, the next few chapters

uncovered many more hidden truths about the family and how they treated Prabha. Each day had become awful for her in the house. Even the kids followed their parents and behaved in an impolite manner with her. Nobody considered her as a human being. She was not allowed to leave the house. She was confined in the four walls of the house for months. The only solace she found was in the privacy of her room at night. Her life had turned absolutely excruciating.

Most of the other pages narrated similar situations for her. Then Dilip arrived at a page that described an unusual event. One night, Prabha tried to escape from the house. She was about to unlock the main door, when she was caught by one of the women in the family. She shouted and all others woke up from sleep. They grabbed her by her hair and brought her back to her room. The two women abused her. They stripped her naked in front of the men in the house and had beaten her mercilessly. She was left locked in her room without food and water that night. Prabha was bleeding. Her left elbow was aching a lot, which was a clear indication that there was probably a hairline fracture.

Dilip recollected that he already had heard about that incident from Prabha the previous night. She had mentioned that she never tried to escape again after the experience during that horrific night. Reading the same in the diary only validated the information. Dilip continued to the next page. As per the date on the top, it was the very next day. Prabha was still locked in the room. In spite of pleading a lot, nobody unlocked the door. She was still bleeding. She was still starving and was thirsty too.

Dilip was not unaware of these events. Still, he was feeling a rush of anger within him. He took a few quick puffs of his *bidi* and threw it to the corner of the room. There was a small pile of butts of *bidi* in the room already. He then focussed on the next chapter. Prabha was writing for three consecutive days. It was the third night after the incident. She wrote that she continued to remain locked in the room for over forty-eight hours. She was too weak to stand on her feet. She was miserably hungry and thirsty. Her elbow was already swollen, and she was unable to move her arm due to a sharp pain. No one entered her room in last three days. No one cared to provide her with food or water. It seemed the entire family was busy in their everyday chores. At times, the entire house was becoming silent, which meant that they were going out keeping her locked in the room. Prabha tried to break the door but she did not have enough strength to do that with only one hand. Shouting a couple of times did not help as there was hardly any chance for anyone to hear her voice from outside. Her room had no direct opening to reach the outside world.

Dilip turned the page. The next page was blank. He turned to the next one. No content was there as well. He quickly flipped through the rest of the notebook. All the subsequent pages were left blank. Dilip sat like a statue on the ground for a few seconds, trying to figure out why Prabha stopped writing abruptly! He quickly went back to the date of the last page Prabha had written. It was a little more than one month old. What happened next? Why did Prabha never write after that night? When and how was she released from that confinement? MOREOVER, WHERE DID SHE DISAPPEAR LAST NIGHT FROM THE LOCKED HOUSE???

Dilip was unable to think. He tried to clear the clutter in his mind. His mind simply refused to work any longer. Dilip looked at the watch. It was evening already. The Kumar family was supposed to come back by the evening. 'They have probably already discovered that their maid is gone. They must have already seen the broken net and the locks and realised that someone had entered their house in their absence.' Dilip thought. He felt a strong desire to run back to that house and ask those people – "Where is Prabha? What did you do to her?" Unfortunately, the only thing he could do was to sit on the ground gazing at the floor with blank eyes, absolutely dumbfounded.

*

In the meantime, the Kumar brothers returned from the local Police station after lodging a complaint about the intrusion in their house while they were out on vacation for five days and four nights. Their fond memories of the vacation were no longer pleasant, after the extremely unpleasant situation they faced immediately on return. Someone breaking into the house and leaving without stealing even a spoon was not only uncomfortable for them but was also hard for the Police officer to believe. The Police officer they reported the occurrence to, promised to pay a visit to the house the next morning to investigate further. The two men sat in the car silently while driving back home. They were not sure what exactly was making them feel uneasy – the suspicious intrusion or the expected visit by the Police officer the next morning.

56

Chapter 10

The Decision

Dilip stayed up the entire night. He anxiously waited for the morning. He needed to dig deeper to find the fact before he could take the final decision. He kept his calm and finished his simple morning meal with bread and tea. Then he sat quietly and smoked a *bidi*. The local markets generally opened around 9 A.M. in the town. There was a need now for him to visit the local market in the vicinity of the Kumar's residence. Local people always proved useful to collect more information.

Dilip left home around nine in the morning to reach the local market near the Kumar's residence. The ideal time to carry out his informal investigation was when most of the shops in the lane were open and business was in full pace. Nobody would have time to notice the activities of an ordinary looking guy with no special physical feature, at one corner of the lane.

Dilip stood around twenty metres away from the Kumar's house. The windows were open today. That meant Kumar family was already back home last night, as he had information about. There was no one around the windows though. Prabha's room could not be seen from outside. There was no point standing there and wasting time. As he was about to turn back, a Police officer entered the lane riding a motorcycle. A Police Constable, at least that is what it looked like from the uniform, was sitting on the back seat. The officer stopped in front of Dilip and asked, "Hey, do you know which one is Praveen Kumar's house?"

Dilip was not prepared for this surprise. It took him few seconds to digest the unexpected situation. "I...I am not local. I don't really know", Dilip fumbled as he spoke.

The police officer was about to say something, when the constable sitting at the back spoke up loudly, "Sir, there it is, 14B." The number of the house was engraved on a piece of stone beside the main door of the house. The officer, wearing dark sunglasses, looked at the direction in which the constable raised his finger at. They did not pause. The officer immediately accelerated on his bike with a loud sound and reached the main door of the house. Dilip was still in shock. He did not wait there any longer. It was not safe to keep standing and watching anymore. By now, he knew that the visit by the Police officer to the Kumars' residence was definitely as a result of his intrusion.

As Dilip started walking away from the house, he turned back one last time. He saw that someone had already opened the door. The face of the person inside could not be seen, but likely it was a woman. The inspector spoke a few words that could not be heard from the distance Dilip was standing at. Then, the duo entered the house and the door was closed behind them. Dilip did not stand there for another moment. His heart-beat already rose to an alarming pace. It was not surprising to him that those guys had already reported to the Police. However, it was frightening to meet the worst nightmare of a thief face to face; that too without any prior notice. It was not a pleasant feeling to know that the Police had already arrived; and soon, they would be looking out for him. He felt cold sweat rolling down his forehead.

Dilip was scared but did not leave the locality immediately. He still had some work to do there. He stopped at a local *paan* shop and smoked a cigarette. The taste of a cigarette felt so good after a long time. The nicotine always did magic to the mind. He casually started chatting with the *Bhaiya* at the paan shop. That guy was busy putting *kaththa* on *paan,* as if he was spreading butter on a piece of bread.

Dilip started a conversation with him in as much normal tone as possible, "What is the Police doing at the Kumar's place?" He tried to keep his breathing and voice under control. Also, he pretended as if he was from the same *galli* and knew Kumars very well.

The shop owner did not look up, but said, "These guys went out on a vacation. There was no one in the house for five days. I heard that some people tried to break in."

Dilip was confused. He was searching for words. He took few more quick puffs and said, "I heard they had a maid. Did they take her along with them to the vacation?"

The *paanwala* replied, "They had a maid. It seems she ran away a month back. Nobody saw her since then."

Dilip paused for a few moments to think. Then he continued, "Are you sure? She might be still in the house."

Now he looked at Dilip and said, "My brother works for them in the garden they have in their backyard. He went there two weeks back and no maid was there. Her name was Prabha. She left the job and the house already. Also, how could she be in, when they locked the house and left for vacation?"

Dilip was about to exclaim, "I MET HER TWO DAYS BACK INSIDE THAT HOUSE…! THEY LOCKED THEIR MAID IN THE HOUSE AND LEFT FOR THE VACATION." but he controlled himself.

Dilip finished his cigarette and threw the butt on the road. He preferred not to extend the conversation beyond this point. Additional words were not going to solve the puzzle. Instead, it might reveal hidden secrets and put him in trouble. He took the change from the *paanwala* and slowly walked away from the *paan* shop without spending one more minute.

*

He was unable to believe what he heard at the *paan* shop. He was still searching for answers to many questions – Where did Prabha disappear inexplicably? Did she leave the notebook on the floor deliberately? If yes, when did she do that? Why did she stop writing abruptly? Did she want him to read it and extend his help? Those questions were already playing around in his mind since last two days.

In addition, now he had a new equation to solve – who met Dilip inside the house if Prabha left one month back? And if that was Prabha, why Kumars were spreading that their maid had already gone long back! After the *paan* shop, Dilip inquired in similar fashion with two more local shop owners in that lane. Everybody said that very rarely Prabha used to come out of the house. Once in a blue moon she used to accompany the two women from the Kumar's family to the local market. She never came out of the house alone. However, since more than last one month nobody had seen her; not even with the Kumar *Bhabis.*

Dilip was unable to think any longer, with all the information jumbled up in his mind. He picked up the diary that was lying on the *khatiya.* He flipped the pages and took out Prabha's photo again, completely lost in his thoughts. He stared at the photo for a few seconds. A voice within him had been telling him since last night that something was very wrong there. He knew that something was being covered up. When he talked to the local people in the morning, he had a feeling that what was visible to the outside world, was not the truth. Lot more were under the water than what was above the surface, like an iceberg.

He kept thinking for a few more moments. Slowly, his eyes brightened. Finally, he was able to make up his mind. His brain and heart were no longer at conflict. The only way he could find the truth, was by involving the Police. However, he was very much aware of the concomitant consequence of reaching out to the Police. He was a thief, and he was guilty of breaking into the house. In fact, he was guilty of breaking into many other houses. He needed to surrender and tell the entire story. The police were already involved in the case, but with a purpose to find the intruder. If Dilip surrendered and described all that he knew to the Police, they would have a bigger purpose and a diverted investigation to find out the whereabouts of an unfortunate maid, who met him twice and mysteriously vanished from the house. The Police would come to know about the dirty secrets of the Kumar family and their merciless treatment of the lady.

The way to police station was actually a one way route for him to uncover the truth about Prabha. Once he was in, there was no way out for him, even if the Police would find out Prabha and proved the Kumars guilty of torturing her for months. In spite of knowing the definitive fate waiting for him, Dilip was determined to sacrifice his freedom to dig the truth out.

Chapter 11

The Interrogation

Dilip was sitting inside a small cell in the Police station, with two other ugly-looking guys. He had reached the police station in the morning with Prabha's diary in hand. He stood in front of the building hesitantly for a few minutes. He lit one last cigarette and smoked really slowly. The nicotine in his brain gave him some strength. Finally, he threw the butt on the ground and stomped on it. Then he walked slowly towards the police station. He entered through the door and walked straight to a Police Constable sitting at an old-fashioned wooden table at one corner of the room. He was then taken to the Senior Officer. Finally, he surrendered and handed over the diary to the inspector. He narrated the entire story to the Inspector and the Constable, sitting in a small, dark confession room filled with a peculiar odour. Now, the cell he was sitting in, was actually worse than the confession room. There was an open toilet at one corner. The cell with iron grills and dampness on the walls was filled with a mixed smell of urine and sweat. "This is called Hell", Dilip thought. This was the hell Dilip always desperately stayed away from. And today he walked into the "Hell" himself, in spite of knowing that he had nothing to gain but would definitely to lose everything.

*

Inspector Siddheshwar Pandey, who was popularly known as Sid, was a short guy of mid-forties. His wide shoulders, dark black moustache and a rough appearance complemented the name that really sounded heavy. Sid had been reading the diary he got from Dilip since morning. It was not that he did not have any other important case in hand, but somehow Dilip's story generated some interest in his mind. The Maid's disappearance from the Kumar's locked residence seemed worth investing some time for. At least there was no harm in spending some time reading the diary.

There was one more reason for Pandey's curiosity about the case. When he visited Kumar's residence a day before, Dlip was the guy he asked for the exact location of Kumar's residence. Pandey was immediately able to recognise Dilip's face as he walked in the Police station in the morning. He did not believe that to be a mere coincidence. He knew that the same guy was moving around Kumar's house aimlessly the other day; and now he surrendered with a statement that he broke into the same house three days back. Pandey was now determined to find the connection and establish an appropriate equation.

He finally finished reading the last page written in the notebook. Rest of the pages were empty as he flipped through those. The missing girl, or whoever wrote this in reality, decided to create some mystery with the abrupt end. "Now why the hell this fellow surrendered!!! Is he out of his mind?" Sid murmured to himself. Then he pushed the book into the right pocket of this *khaki* trouser and got up from his chair. He shouted in his typical North Indian Accent, "Oye Gupta, *gaddi* nikal".

Gupta's appearance was in stark contrast to that of inspector Pandey. Constable Sudhir Gupta was a tall, dark but not at all handsome guy of mid-thirties. As of now, he was the most obedient right hand for Pandey. Gupta was playing games on his smartphone. He immediately got up from his chair, put his smartphone in the pocket, and ran for the Police jeep. Pandey was already there before he could reach the jeep. Gupta believed that inspector Pandey always reached everywhere before Gupta intentionally, just to make him embarrassed. Probably it was Pandey's way to prove seniority, and thus, superiority, in everything they did together. In Gupta's opinion, Inspector Pandey had some kind of superiority complex. Gupta stared at Pandey's face and without a single word he got into the driver's seat of the Police jeep.

*

"The thief who broke into your house, surrendered today at the Police station", Pandey started speaking with a mouth full of *pan masala*. Praveen, Naveen, Sarita and Deepa were sitting on the sofa in the drawing room. Pandey was on a couch with Gupta standing right beside him. The Kumars did not expect this news to come. They reported to the Police station, without any hope of the intruder getting caught. People do go to Police stations to file reports; but how many are actually resolved so fast!

Pandey continued, "This fellow is a petty thief. He breaks into houses to steal. He tracked that you guys were off for a vacation and just took chances. You said nothing was stolen, is that right?" Naveen replied, "Not really…I mean…not something we could figure out."

Pandey kept silence for a few seconds, staring at Naveen. Then he said, "Do you have a maid who works here".

Pandey kept looking at Kumar brothers, waiting for a response. The two brothers looked at each other. Naveen fumbled a little, "Yes, we had. But she is gone now. She left a month back." It was clear that the question seemed completely unrelated to the issue at hand to them.

Pandey frowned a little. Then his eyes rolled on to Praveen. Pandey asked, "When did you guys say that she had left?" Though Pandey was looking at Praveen, Naveen responded again, "A month ago; actually, a little over a month to be accurate."

"What was her name? You people never mentioned about a maid when I came for the first time!" Pandey asked.

"Prabha", a short answer came from Naveen. Then he added, "but why are we even talking about our maid? There was no reason to mention about our maid. You came for an investigation about the intrusion in our house."

Pandey remained silent for a few moments. Then he inserted his palm into the pocket of his trouser and took out the small notebook. He dropped the notebook with a moderately loud sound on the centre table. Everybody's eyes were glued to the book. Pandey broke the silence as he continued speaking, "The burglar submitted this diary to the Police station. He claimed that he met your domestic help inside this house just three days back, when he broke in. Apparently, this diary was written by Prabha, your maid, during her stint in your house."

Now Praveen opened his mouth after long. He started with an uneasy smile on his lips, "This is impossible. Prabha does not stay here now. Who is that guy…I want to see! That scoundrel must be telling a big lie to you Inspector."

"But the diary may not be telling a lie Sir!", Pandey replied almost immediately. Then he kept talking, "Even if I believe that the girl left a month back, she definitely did not have a pleasant experience in association with you guys. At least, that is what the diary reveals".

Praveen almost exclaimed, "We don't know about this diary. This must be a trick planned by the guy you caught. He must be having some intention behind all these. What's the name of that fellow?"

"His name is Dilip…do you guys know him? Or, do you know if Prabha knew him?" Pandey asked.

"We don't know anyone named Dilip. Also, how are we supposed to know if Prabha knew him! She is gone…chapter closed," Praveen finished the entire sentence without a pause.

Pandey raised his eyebrows and said, "I thought you would ask about what the diary has. But it seems you people are not interested to know the details. However, it is my responsibility to tell you all that are written here. Then you may see if you can recollect anything."

*

Pandey started narrating the content of the notebook in brief to the Kumars. He did not read each page but tried to narrate with as much detail as possible. As he spoke, the expressions on their faces were gradually changing. By the time he was done, there was a mixed expression of surprise and incredulity on everybody's face in the room. Praveen spoke again, "These are not true. This can't be true. I don't even believe that the girl wrote a diary. This must be a plan by the fellow in your custody."

Before Pandey could figure out how to confront; for the first time, one of the ladies spoke. Sarita said in a calm voice, "Inspector *Saab*, all that are written in the diary are absolutely untrue and whoever has planned this must be an imposter. We never treated our maid that way. We are a respectable family staying in this locality for over fifteen years. Nobody ever complained about our behaviour and treatment of people."

She paused a little to think something. Then she added, "Also, I am sure you would not consider this diary as an evidence against us, simply based on assumptions! This content can't be accepted as there is no proof that these are true and there is also no owner of the diary."

Pandey looked surprised. He responded with sarcasm

in his voice, "You are already running ahead of me Ma'am. I can't believe we are already discussing about evidence. What's wrong…where is Prabha?"

Sarita's voice was more assertive this time, almost to the level of rudeness, "Nothing is wrong inspector. As you already are accusing us of torturing our maid on the basis of the ownerless diary with some junk content in it, I felt it was important to make it clear that these don't make any sense at all. Secondly, we have no idea where Prabha is at this moment as we are not in touch with her since she had left the work."

Pandey smiled a little. Still sceptic, he said, "One last question as of now – why did Prabha leave?"

Deepa replied in a polite manner to reduce the effect of apparent impoliteness of Sarita, "Sir, now-a-days maids rarely stay in one house for over two years. We consider ourselves fortunate that this one stayed that long. She asked for more money, which we could not afford. So, very likely she left ours looking for another work with a better wage."

Pandey was definitely not convinced but he did not have anything to counter that statement. He got up from his place and said curtly, "One more time, I want to see the place through which the guy broke into the house."

Chapter 12

The Confusion

Pandey did not directly come back to the Police station from the Kumar's residence. He visited few shop owners around the house. Two of them were the owners of the two shops on the ground floor of the same building. Another one was the same *paan shop* owner that Dilip also had spoken to earlier. Gupta was sent to have a chat with that guy. One information they received consistently from all three was that the maid, Prabha, used to work at the Kumar's place. She was very rarely seen outside the house. Local people saw her only a few times in last two years, when she accompanied one of the two ladies from the family to the local market to carry the vegetable baskets home. However, none of them had seen Prabha in last one month. In fact, the two shop owners echoed the same information that the Kumar family had already provided - Prabha left the work without any prior notice about a month back.

In a nutshell, all statements by everyone indicated that Prabha was there in the house; and now she was nowhere to be seen since over a month. To contradict that information, Dilip had already claimed to have met her just a few days back in the house when he entered the building from the backyard with an intention of burglary. Seemingly Dilip was partly telling the truth. At least, that's what Pandey had concluded. One of all the fingerprints collected from the house matched with Dilip's. The rest of the fingerprints were of the family members. That proved Dilip's entry into the house. His fingerprints were found even in Prabha's room and on the broken locks. The only places Dilip apparently did not visit were the bedrooms of the two families. Therefore, Dilip's claim of meeting Prabha was the only part that was still in dark.

Generally, Pandey never bothered about collecting fingerprints for a petty crime like what Dilip did. Nonetheless, this case was different. Here a thief entered a house and left without stealing even a spoon. Then the same guy surrendered to the Police station and claimed to have met a girl in the house, who left five weeks back. To complicate it further, the thief also mentioned about disappearance of the woman on the third night when he entered the house again. And then Dilip surrendered with a notebook that told nasty stories. Ghastly murder mysteries seemed to be less complicated than the case at hand.

This time when Pandey visited the Kumars' house again, he stood in front of the iron mesh and examined the hole closely. The hole was big enough for an adult with a thin body to go through with some effort. When he was done, he had asked, "And where is Prabha's room?"

Naveen had led the way to the maid's room. Pandey, constable Gupta and everybody else followed. Pandey entered the small and shabby room that had absolutely no furniture. There was a thin layer of dust on the floor. It was evident that the room was not in use for at least a month. The only window, which was significantly small to call a window, opened to the corridor inside the house. There was no connection of that room with the outside world. More than that, there was not much to observe in the room. Pandey looked around for more. He was visibly disappointed that day. Lack of evidence always was disappointing for him.

After closely scrutinizing every corner of the room, Pandey and Gupta entered all other rooms in the house. Pandey took note of a few observations. Finally, he had asked Gupta to arrange someone to collect fingerprints in order to match with Dilip's. Pandey was still not sure if Dilip was the one who really had entered the house. There was a possibility that he was cooking stories with some other intention. There were chances that he knew the maid and had come back now with some other bigger motive. His statement was yet to be validated.

Now, with all the fingerprints collected and matched, that link had been established. The story of a petty thief did not interest him. Now there was a new angle of a "missing" maid; at least as per Dilip's version. Pandey was not sure what to believe, but he was putting constant effort to sniff something bigger and more significant.

*

Pandey sat face to face to Dilip. Dilip was already scared. He had never faced an interrogation earlier in his life. He always stayed away from Police. An officer like Pandey was probably too harsh to deal with; at least for a criminal who saw a lock-up for the first time in life. Every time Pandey interrogated Dilip in last few days, he felt a dry throat and wobbly legs. Fortunately, the inspector did not *spare the rod* yet, but he was breathlessly waiting for something bad to happen.

Pandey opened his mouth first, "I am asking for one last time. What do you want? Why are you doing all these?"

Definitely this was not the first time Dilip was asked this question. From day two of his arrest, the inspector had been trying to know the real intention behind Dilip's surrender. Now Dilip was tired of repeating the same story. However, he was not surprised. When he decided to surrender, he was more or less prepared for the consequences. He knew that the Kumars were not going to accept the allegations. He knew from the neighbours that Prabha apparently left the house long back. He also knew that he met a lady of flesh and blood, who claimed to be Prabha, inside the house just a few days back. The only answers he did not know was where the girl vanished and why she left the diary in the room.

Pandey yelled in a deep loud voice, "How long will you stay mum, you ******?"

Dilip shuddered. For the first time he realised he was not a tough guy at all. He had a soft interior under a rough and apparently hard façade.

Dilip's hands were trembling, voice unsteady. He also started stammering, "Sir…sir, I only know that I met a girl in the house. I…I had no other intention than stealing. I had told you that I entered the house thinking it was empty. I did not even know that the girl was there." Dilip paused.

Pandey shouted again, "I have heard these a number of times already. If you met her, where did she go? Secondly, the Kumars are saying the girl left over a month back. Then how did she meet you? Her ghost came in to welcome you?"

Dilip looked around. There was no water bottle anywhere. He did not have the courage to ask for water. He swallowed his own saliva to keep his throat wet. He was not seeing any way to prove his innocence. Moreover, there was no way to prove that he really met someone, who later disappeared.

Pandey continued, "I am sure you used to know Prabha already. And you came back with some intention to extract money from the family with these false allegations. I already asked a number of people who know the family well. There was no maid in the house; not at least when you got in."

Pandey finished all the sentences breathlessly. Then he paused for a moment. Then he added, "Now you need to tell me who wrote the diary and why. I am not buying your story of a tortured maid stuck in the house, who then evaporated like a pinch of camphor in the air. Even the gardener who worked for the Kumars on regular basis did not see their maid when he last visited them a few weeks back. We have already talked to many other people."

Dilip looked at the sky helplessly. There was no sky. It was only dirty and shabby ceiling above, full of spider nets. Who would want to believe a burglar like Dilip! He had no solid proof as evidence to establish the facts.

Pandey already examined the writing on the diary. It did not match with Dilip's writing. As the maid was not around, there was hardly any way to find out if she had written the diary. Pandey continued, "Don't waste my time. The diary proves nothing. It does not even have an owner. In case you thought of putting that family in trouble and then earn some money, that is not going to work."

Dilip remained silent for a while to collect his thoughts. He was already in a mess. He did not have any way out now. That did not matter though. He came prepared. But what did he come here for? Not to prove himself innocent; but to find Prabha. To find the truth. If what was written in the diary was the truth, then those scoundrels deserved to learn a lesson. BUT HOW…HOW…Dilip felt hopeless. His back was against the wall. He had nothing to lose. Suddenly Dilip started feeling more confident. What else the Police could do to him. The worst could be a jail term of a few years.

Dilip's voice became calmer and firm. He said, "Sir, I did not have any intention to extract money. I am ready to face anything. But please do not let them get away with their lies. Find Prabha…please sir…find the girl and prove me wrong."

There was something in his voice that did not let Pandey say anything else. He looked into Dilip's eyes and said, "Better this be true. Else…" Pandey did not complete. He pushed the stool back and got up. Making loud sounds with his Police boots on the floor, he disappeared through the door of the interrogation room.

Chapter 13

The Information

These were the phases in an investigation that Pandey did not like. He was killing time as he neither had any information nor he could prove anything. He was feeling impatient now. One of the two parties were playing games for sure. Either the Kumars were deceptive or Dilip was a liar with some plan in mind. Pandey shouted, "Gupta, come here fast…".

Constable Gupta was at his table outside the room, as usually playing games on his smartphone. He had a feeling that long association with a smartphone could make him smart; or at least smarter than his boss.

Gupta entered the room with the phone in his hand. Pandey continued speaking without even looking up, "Gupta, get your informers involved in the case of the missing maid of the Kumars. Ask them to dig out as much information they can find; small or big. Even if you feel something is irrelevant, do not use your brain. Let me know and I will decide what to do with it."

Now this was something Gupta always hated about Pandey. Pandey was a good guy, but he very often belittled Gupta. He believed this was another strategy Pandey had, just to prove his seniority to him. However, there was no way to revolt.

Pandey did not pay attention to Gupta's expression. He looked up and said, "Also, I want you to do something additional. This diary talked about the village Prabha belonged to. Dilip also mentioned the same name that he heard from the girl. Go to the village tomorrow itself and find if anyone knows Prabha. As per the diary, there should be a distant Aunt Prabha has. Now don't stand here looking at my face. Start early in the morning tomorrow."

Gupta was about to leave the room when Pandey called him back, "Hey, also find out if Dilip is from the same village and if he knew Prabha earlier. Chances are they knew each other, and this is a plan jointly drafted with some specific objective. I won't be surprised if Prabha is hiding in the village while this guy came to the town to create the drama of Prabha's disappearance."

Ali was a local guy. His association with the Police started with getting arrested for petty crimes like pickpocketing in the local trains and selling movie tickets in black. Later, he turned an informer for the Police. He worked for Gupta, the constable. In addition, he started selling movie tickets, but not in the black market. He was now a *ticket executive* at the authorised ticket counter of the same cinema hall, in front of which he used to sell tickets in black.

Ali got a work that Gupta called him for. He was asked to find more information about the Kumar family, their activities outside home, and what else people knew about the maid they had. Gupta also provided him with a copy of Prabha's photograph found inside the diary. Without any delay Ali began his work. He knew the Kumar family members by face.

Since morning Ali had been talking to different people. He was not alone though. He was working for the Police, but he had sub-agents who worked for him. His boys were also deployed for the same work. More people would get more information. Out of all the pieces of data, one or two could come out as relevant information. This was the data collection phase and not the time for analysis. In fact, the informers were not supposed to do analysis. They were expected to only pass on the information to the Police.

Ali spoke to the local shop owners, milkman, newspaper guy, and few of the neighbours. He got nothing different from what the Police already knew. Eventually Ali reached the *paan* shop at the lane of the Kumar's residence. Nobody could overlook that *paanwala's* shop. The location of the shop was so convenient and prominent that people invariably noticed it. Also, from that location anybody could keep a watch on the Kumar's house conveniently, keeping safe distance. Ali found these *panwalas* very informative. They sat in one place, doing the same job throughout the day and gossiping about everything under the sun. Gossips were not always worthless. At times, there were useful pieces of news, that otherwise never surfaced. One had to only keep their eyes and ears open to extract the right matter. Being at the right place, at the right time was the job of an informer. Exactly that is what Ali was trying to do.

*

Constable Gupta reached back to town little late in the evening. He got down at the rail station and reached the parking. His bike was parked there since morning. He started the bike and left for the Police station. Pandey generally worked till late evening. He had no intention to go home as he had no one at home. Probably having no family was the reason for bachelors of Pandey's age being more productive.

However, Gupta had a wife who could make his life difficult if he was late to home. So, he was in a hurry to complete his reporting and go back home. He accelerated on his bike to reach the Police station as soon as possible.

Pandey was still in his room, sipping tea. Gupta entered the room hurriedly. Pandey looked up. He was waiting for Gupta to report. Gupta was still breathing heavily but started talking.

"Sir, I found Prabha's Aunt. Many others in the village knew Prabha. But the girl did not return to the village since she left home. Nobody in the village had seen her in last few years. I inquired with different people." He stopped for air for a few moments. Pandey was silently listening. He patiently waited for more.

Gupta added, "But Sir…nobody knows Dilip in the village. I showed his photo to many people. There was no Dilip ever in the village. So, either this maid got to know Dilip after she came to town, or what Dilip is narrating is correct. But definitely he is not from her village."

Now Pandey asked, "Does her aunt know Prabha was working in the Kumars' house?"

"No Sir, that old lady was not in touch with Prabha after she left her in the town. She only knew the first place where she brought Prabha to. That was a few years back. I have taken the address of that house. I can find the location."

Pandey was in deep thought for some time. For the first time he felt like appreciating Gupta. But he did not show that on his face. He said with his face expression unchanged, "Go there tomorrow. Find out who they were and if Prabha went back to them. Even if she is not there, find out if they can tell about any other place where Prabha could be staying."

Pandey was partly hopeful but not fully happy yet. The information Gupta found did not solve anything. It only meant that Dilip was not entirely telling lies. Prabha's whereabouts still remained a mystery, in case Dilip really had met her in the house.

*

Constable Gupta was about to pick up his backpack from his desk to go back to his usual rotten life, when Ali entered the Police station. There were sparkle in his eyes.

Gupta was familiar with this. This meant Ali managed to find something; at least some information to convey to Pandey for now.

Gupta grabbed Ali's hand and almost dragged him to Pandey's room. He did not have time to listen to the whole story, and then communicate to his boss. Pandey had also got up from his chair already to go back to his so-called home. He looked curiously at Ali. Though Ali worked primarily for the constable, Pandey knew him.

Ali started talking, "Saab, I came to know something unusual. May not be significant but just in case…you know. You can figure out if this is relevant."

"Come to the point Ali. I don't have whole night to sit here", Pandey said.

Ali continued, "Sir I managed to find the guy who worked as a gardener on contract basis for the Kumars. I just had some casual chatter with him."

"Oh, we already met that guy. What's new in it," Gupta commented. Pandey raised one hand to stop Gupta and gestured Ali to continue. He never had much faith on Gupta's interrogation skills. In many cases Pandey spoke to the same people that Constable Gupta already had spoken to and was able to extract more relevant information than Gupta could.

Ali kept talking, "First I asked about the maid. He said that the last time he worked in their backyard was over a month back. That time he saw the maid in the house. The same day they asked this fellow to bring some saplings of seasonal flowers in his next visit. Every year they do the same. The Kumars were very fond of gardening and always kept the backyard well decorated with various plants and flower beds."

"So what?" Pandey was getting impatient.

Ali continued, "So, around two weeks back this guy again reached Kumars' house with the saplings. To his surprise, this time the Kumars were completely disinterested. They refused to let him work in the garden. They said they changed their mind and had no time for gardening. Then the gardener insisted as he had already bought the saplings and they were costly. The Kumars got little annoyed. They were looking anxious. They discussed something amongst themselves and paid him money for the saplings but did not take his service. They were in a hurry to drive him away as soon as possible. That guy had been working for them for many years. It was not something he was expecting. While coming back, he also peeked into the garden and saw that it was dry and almost empty, with almost no plant and flowers left. He was unable to understand the reason for the sudden change in mind."

Ali paused for a few seconds. Pandey waited as he expected a little more; might be something like a closing statement.

After a short breather, Ali said, "That was the last time when he went into the house, and the maid was not there. It looked like she had already left the work."

Chapter 14

The Excavation

All four members of the Kumar family were standing in a row at their backyard. Pandey had arrived with his team consisting of two junior officers, constable Gupta, two lady constables and two other guys who were brought for digging soil in the garden. Of course, Pandey had no plan to start planting trees. However, he already had started to sniff out something very gruesome; something that did not grab his attention before. Nothing was confirmed but it made sense to take a chance. His gut feeling had never betrayed him in his entire career in the Police. So, he decided to explore how strong his sixth sense was.

Pandey did not wait for even a day after hearing the narration from Ali the last evening. The very next morning, he managed to collect a search warrant. Then he arranged his team and left for Kumars' residence. Needless to say that the Kumars did not anticipate this. Pandey had to face a lot of resistance from the family members. The more they argued, the more they threatened him; the more he was convinced that he was on the right track. Now he was waiting eagerly to literally dig out the truth from the ground.

The Kumar family finally stopped resisting. They were now silent and their faces expressionless. The two guys who were brought in by the Police, had already started manual excavation in the small garden. There were not many plants left in the garden. So, it did not take too long to clean the ground and start their work.

There was one more guy who was brought to the spot. That was Dilip. He was standing silently, hands tied with a handcuff. Probably the result of the excavation was going to decide his fate.

*

Just when one starts losing hope, things generally begin looking up. One of the two guys shouted, "Saab, something is in here. Please have a look."

Everybody rushed and surrounded the spot he was delving. A piece of cloth of pale-yellow colour was sticking out of the ground. At the same time a strong pungent smell filled the air around. Pandey was familiar with that odour. Almost everybody covered their mouths with handkerchief. Digging continued. Pandey instructed the soil digger to be careful with his tool. Whatever was inside needed to be extracted as it was, without damage.

Within a few minutes, everything got revealed. Mud and dirt were piled up at one side, as they dug large hole on the ground. A decomposed human body wrapped in a yellow *saree* was lying inside. In fact, a human body would be an overstatement. It almost turned into a skeleton. A very little flesh was left on the open parts of the body such as face, arms and the feet. Face was definitely not recognizable. Traces of moderately long hair were clearly visible. Even without the support of the forensic experts, one could tell that the dead body was of a woman.

This exploration created a temporary chaos among the people present at the spot. One of the two lady constables started puking. Gupta could not stare at it any longer. Pandey was also noticeably disturbed. His face was clearly expressing disgust. Even the guys who were digging the ground were taken aback. Not everybody could digest such a horrifying sight.

While all these were going on, Dilip remained absolutely speechless. He was neither puking, nor covering his mouth or not even looking away. He was dumbstruck, but not due to the terrible condition of the body. He was looking at the *saree* on the dead body, with horror and disbelief in his eyes. THAT…THAT WAS THE *SAME SAREE* THAT PRABHA WAS WEARING WHEN DILIP MET HER IN THE HOUSE. In fact, even on the second day, she wore the same one.

The body was clearly not ten days old. It could be weeks ago when she was buried. Skull and bones were visible as flesh had almost disappeared. However, it was not possible to state the exact age of the dead body. There was one more confirmation required. Nobody knew, except the Kumars, whether the body was actually of their maid, Prabha.

*

The Police needed an official confirmation. Forensic experts were brought in to find out "when" and "how" of the death and illegal burial of the body. The "why" part was Pandey's responsibility to obtain from the Kumar family members. All four were already arrested, sitting in the Police vans. So far, they all remained silent. Everybody's attentions now had turned from Dilip to the Kumars. All localites had gathered in front of the house and the entrance of the lane. Police van, extraction of a dead body, forensic officials – all together was an unforgettable experience for people staying in the small town. They hardly had any thrill in their lives.

Pandey was not a person who would wait for confession. He already sent Gupta back to Prabha's village to bring her old Aunt to the town for identification of the body. She was the only relative who had seen Prabha till her adulthood. However, at the same time, he was not much hopeful of that process. The face and the body were definitely not in right condition to be identified as Prabha. But a process was a process. And Pandey always followed the process.

Slowly the body was collected in a zipped bag specially designed for these purposes. A van was called in for taking the body to the department for post-mortem. Forensic and fingerprint experts were working all over the house and in the garden. The house was announced to be sealed by the Police. A photographer was at work. The children of the Kumars were handed over to their closest relatives. They might be questioned later, following the right procedure. All in all, it was a typical crime scene that people had seen only in movies.

Dilip was also taken back to the Police jeep. He also had a lot of questions to answer. He was the last person who claimed to meet Prabha approximately ten days back. Now, Pandey was dealing with a dead body that was a lot more than ten days old. However, in spite of all the disorder and confusion, Pandey was still feeling slightly cheerful inside. After all, his intuition did not go in vain. He was actually feeling proud of himself, but that was not the time to celebrate. A lot of answers were yet to be found.

Pandey entered the jeep and sat opposite to Dilip. He looked into Dilip's eyes and said, "Look Dilip, you mentioned that you saw Prabha around early last week. Are you still sticking to the same statement?".

Dilip did not say anything but just nodded his head in affirmation. Pandey waited for a few seconds and then said, "We still don't know if this is Prabha. If yes, then one thing I can tell right away from my experience. This body is at least over a month old. My guess would be that this lady died at least thirty to forty days back. Even if I believe that this is Prabha, how come you met her last week? Are you understanding that there is a big gap?

Pandey was about to say something additional, when he saw a junior officer approaching the jeep, with a medium sized, partly broken suitcase in his hand. He was looking excited. He dropped the suitcase in front of Pandey and said, "Sir, our guys also found this beside the body. One of us saw the handle and we got the whole thing pulled out after digging a little further. This is full of women's clothes. So, I wanted to inform you."

Pandey got down from the car and observed the suitcase closely. It was covered with mud, stinking terribly. Pandey covered his mouth with his handkerchief and slightly opened the suitcase with the other hand. There were apparently *sarees, blouses and undergarments,* all jumbled up in an untidy way. It looked like someone forced everything inside the suitcase in a hurry. The condition of the suitcase and the clothes were really bad due to remaining under the ground for a long time.

Pandey closed the suitcase and gave necessary instructions to the officer to collect that as an evidence. Then he turned to Dilip and said, "There will be investigation on the Kumars. They will pay for what they have done. But you owe an explanation to me about how you met her when she was already six feet under. Did you already know about this murder?"

Panday waited for an answer but Dilip remained silent. He seemed to be in a different world, aloof from everything else.

Pandey was going to walk away, when Dilip opened his mouth, "Sir…".

Pandey stopped and turned back inquisitively. He was either expecting more information or a confession.

Dilip looked up at Pandey and said, "When I met Prabha, she was wearing the same *saree* that we saw today on the dead body. Also, I saw that suitcase earlier in Prabha's room, when I went into the house the second time."

Chapter 15

The Last Encounter

Constable Gupta came back from Prabha's village by the evening. He found Prabha's aunt and brought her along with him. The Police then took the woman to the morgue for identification of the body. The woman had a predictable reaction as she was brought to the partially decomposed corpse with very little amount of skin and flesh left only on some parts. It was free from mud as it was cleaned by the forensic experts for examination, but still there was an acrid smell. Unfortunately, the lady could not tell anything definitive. It was not possible to identify the body in such condition. She was only severely shocked to see the body as she had never had such a horrifying experience.

However, she was able to identify some of the clothes that were collected, including the one that was on the body. In addition, he could instantly recognize the suitcase that was found beside the corpse. Now there was no doubt that it definitely belonged to Prabha. She had carried all her belongings in the same suitcase when she was brought to the town by her Aunt.

In the meantime, the post-mortem report came to the Police. The body was found to be around forty days old, as Pandey had guessed. Unfortunately, the cause of death was not very clear as the body had decayed significantly. It was too late to conclusively detect the reason for her death. The experts could only confirm that it was of a woman in her mid-thirties.

*

The Kumars had lost their courage and ability to resist any longer. The two brothers, Praveen and Naveen, opened their mouths first. Following the two men, even the two ladies agreed to confess. They gave in to the pressure built on them by all the findings. They were not seasoned criminals after all.

All results and reports had almost cleared the cloud. Though the Police could not find a solid proof that the dead body was of the maid, the Kumars were still required to explain the one month old corpse found in their backyard. "We don't know anything," was not an acceptable answer anymore.

Everything was recorded, as all four family members confessed to the Police. Their confession also matched with the diary. It explicitly answered the abrupt ending of Prabha's writing.

The Kumars accepted the allegations of physical and mental torture on the maid for a duration of almost two years. Around forty days back, on a particular night, Prabha attempted an escape from the house. Sarita had coincidentally come out of her bedroom at that time to attend nature's call. Prabha was trying to open the main door but that made a lot of noise. Sarita heard the sound and alerted everybody. Prabha was caught. She was forcibly brought back to her room. She was brutally tortured by all four members of the family. Following that, she remained locked in the room for next three days. Nobody showed any mercy. She kept crying and begging for water. She was completely ignored and left unattended. After three days in a row, she stopped pleading. There was no sound of her any longer from the room, which created an alarm. The Kumars opened the door and found her lying on the floor. Apparently, it looked like she was unconscious. When they closely checked, her pulse was missing. She was not breathing anymore.

They were scared. They did not intend to kill her but wanted to just teach a lesson. Unfortunately, there was no way to get her checked by a doctor. They could end up in jail for beating the girl and illegally keeping her in captivity. In case she was dead, the consequence could have been the worst. But then, it was not possible to take the girl out and dump somewhere else. They could have been easily noticed by the neighbours. So, they all found a way to cover up the entire mess before the sunrise; before the world woke up.

The Kumars decided to take advantage of the garden in their backyard. The two brothers dug up a hole big enough to contain the body of the girl, in the darkness of the night. The isolated position of the house and the high walls around the garden made it easier for them to complete their task, without raising any suspicion among the people around. Since then, she remained buried in the Kumars' garden. The most inhuman part of the story was that when Prabha was buried, there was no confirmation that she was already dead.

The confession provided answers to many questions the Police had been struggling with. It explained why the gardener was not allowed to work in the backyard, whereas he was previously asked by the Kumars to bring some seasonal plants and flowers for planting in their garden. It also explained why they made the story that the maid had left the work one month back and why nobody in the area had seen the woman even for a single time in the last few weeks. In addition, it clarified why at the Police station the Kumars reported a suspected intrusion during their absence but never talked about their maid going missing, when they came back from the vacation.

However, the confession did not explicate two things that kept everyone still in dark. In fact, the mystery turned darker and horrifying without those missing links.

Firstly, The Kumars mentioned that they found Prabha's diary in her room when she was buried. They threw her suitcase along with her body in the garden but actually had *burnt* the diary into ashes in order to completely destroy the only record of their misdeed. Probably that was the reason that they believed the diary to be an attempt by Dilip to expose them. In one hand, they thought that it was recreated by Dilip as he might have got to know about the crime they committed. They suspected that Dilip knew Prabha and had been trying to take revenge on them. On the other, they were worried that there might be a second diary or a copy of the one they had already burnt, that somehow reached Dilip.

Secondly, nobody could ever believe that Dilip met the dead woman inside the house. The Kumars never allowed the maid to go out of the house alone. Therefore, the chance of her meeting Dilip was negligible. Also, Dilip was not from Prabha's village. Even the other houses where Prabha worked could not throw any light on a possible hidden relationship between the two. That did not invalidate the possibility that they knew each other though; but lack of information did not provide a logical answer about how Dilip knew Prabha and how he accessed the diary that was destroyed already.

*

Dilip still stuck to his initial statement. He refused the possibility of having prior information about the unintentional murder and illegal burial of Prabha's body. Everyone involved with the case was left perplexed realizing that when Dilip broke into the house, Prabha was already dead and buried in the backyard. Police had been still trying to understand how Dilip could meet Prabha twice inside the house.

However, the revelations freed up Dilip of the charges of being involved in the woman's mysterious disappearance or a possible murder of the victim. Dilip was not bothered about his acquittal though. He remained in a state of shock. He only knew that he met Prabha in the same yellow *saree* that was found on the corpse. He knew that Prabha did not vanish from the house but actually was already in a different world. AND *the last encounter* that he had, could have only one explanation of everything that he got inadvertently entangled with – through Dilip, Prabha had taken her vengeance on the people who ill-treated her and left her to die painfully.

Dilip was released few weeks later in the light of the confession the Kumar family had already made, leaving no solid evidence against him. However, he left burglary and could never gather the courage to go in an empty house again. He almost lost his mental stability. He started seeing a figure of a woman in a dark tunnel in his dreams. He was now afraid of darkness.

What Critics Say for "The Last Encounter"

The mystery elements find their ways in the fragment of human lives, whether they are in fiction or reality. When this is narrated the right way, it can keep the readers involved and engaged throughout their reading of the book. In his book, Abhishek Roy Chowdhury, "The Last Encounter," packs his book with the same elements of mystery and presents the events in a nail-biting form for the readers to keep them both wondering and glued to the action of the book. This is a major attraction that makes the book an immediate page-turner for readers, and they can't help but get fixated on the text from the moment they go through the first few pages.

The short novel begins in a relatively conventional style where the author patiently takes his time to build up the plot around the protagonist and weave it in the light of the events that his life comprises of. At the same time, he shows life from the other side of a social group who have to opt for unfair means to earn their living and provide two square meals per day. Mostly told in the third person narration, the readers are more like observers, learning and understanding the life of the protagonist, Dilip, with close observation. He may be into thieving by profession, but clearly, the readers do not see him or judge him with eyes of prejudice or hatred.

As the plot unfolds, the idea of thieving takes a back seat, and other significant matters take center stage, and the readers' minds are also occupied with them after that.

Prabha's diary may have all the answers that the readers and Dilip have, yet the author cleverly holds to their curiosity by leaving loopholes which they can only fill up once they read till the last page. In all manners, Prabha's diary emerges as one significant for both the police investigation and the readers' understanding of the atrocities she went through. How she appears creates an air of mystery, and the discovery of her diary only further heightens the puzzle the author had already built around her character.

The author constructs the plot with careful clarity. If readers do not read the blurb, they cannot have the slightest clue of the direction in which the action would go or where the narrative is headed towards. This altogether helps create a well-knit plot where the story would unfold only when the readers would read through the book from cover to cover. Dilip's character has different dimensions, which overshadow the fact that he is in the negative profession of thieving. His concern for Prabha shows the humanitarian element in his personality and reinforces that a person's work or job cannot define their temperament. When the readers see the Kumar family in sharp contrast in light of their social behavior and their lifestyle, they forget the facts related to Dilip altogether.

"The Last Encounter" features a story that is written in a span of around 100 pages. In addition to the mysterious plot, which features more of joining the dots situations, the author presents different themes that form the heart of majority of Indian households. The first and foremost theme is the circumstances that force people to take professions that would otherwise not be everyone's first choice. Other themes include people's hypocritical behavior, their double standards, the attitude towards domestic help even though they are equally as human as anyone else, the absence of giving basic dignity and respect to a person, and the fact that how the economic position of a person can define just anything in a person's life. These factors loom large when the Kumar family comes into the picture and beyond mere mentions of others.

Prabha represents the many women who suffer like her in silence, with failed attempts in protesting against the wrongs done to her. Dilip and Prabha are more or less two sides of the same coin, which show society's faces, which are defined by their gender. Readers who are interested in reading books that have the potential to bring out the detective in them should try reading "The Last Encounter." There may not be an actual detective presence in the book yet. As the police investigation comes into force, the readers also become individual investigators trying to unravel and unveil the secrets surrounding Prabha's character.

The author keeps the language simple and clear; the plot development is specific, focused and driven at an accurate speed to keep the readers in tune with the action. All readers interested in reading content that is short, sharp, and thought-provoking can read Chowdhury's work without any second thoughts.

Reviewed By:
-   **Akhila Saroha**

The Literature Today

www.ingramcontent.com/pod-product-compliance
Lightning Source LLC
Chambersburg PA
CBHW021956170726
47994CB00021B/817